The Boxcar Children Mysteries

THE ZOMBIE PROJECT

created by
GERTRUDE CHANDLER WARNER

Illustrated by Robert Papp

ALBERT WHITMAN & Company
Chicago, Illinois

Library of Congress Cataloging-in-Publication Data
is available from the Library of Congress.

The Zombie Project
Created by Gertrude Chandler Warner;
Illustrated by Robert Papp.

ISBN: 978-0-8075-9492-6 (hardcover)
ISBN: 978-0-8075-9493-3 (paperback)

Cover art by Robert Papp.

For information about Albert Whitman & Company,
visit our web site at www.albertwhitman.com.

Contents

THE ZOMBIE PROJECT

CHAPTER 1

Did You Say Zombie?

Whoo-ooh! Six-year-old Benny stirred in his sleep as an owl hooted in the distance.

The owl flew on silent wings and landed in a tree outside the cabin window. *Whoo-ooh!*

Benny opened his eyes. Why was that owl hooting so loudly?

Benny sat up in bed and looked around. Henry, his fourteen-year-old brother, was still asleep.

A light flashed in the cabin window and then disappeared. Benny got out of bed.

Twelve-year-old Jessie and ten-year-old Violet were asleep in their room on the other side of the small cabin.

Benny looked out the window into the woods. A light flickered and flashed in the darkness. Benny watched as the light moved farther away and then disappeared.

It looks like those people found their cabin, thought Benny. *And here we are in ours.* Benny went back to bed and pulled the covers up to his chin. The cabin reminded him of the boxcar. He closed his eyes and drifted off to sleep.

* * * *

"Wake up, sleepyhead," said Jessie.

"Rise and shine," said Henry. "We want to go to breakfast."

Benny sat up right away. "Breakfast!"

"I told you that was the magic word," said Violet.

Henry, Jessie, and Violet laughed. They knew how much Benny loved to eat.

"I'll be outside with the new camera," said Violet. She held the camera decorated with purple stars in her hand. The camera could take photos *and* videos. Grandfather Alden had bought it for all of them, but Violet was the artistic one. She loved the color purple and loved taking photos and making videos.

"Let me come with you," said Jessic.

"We'll find you when Benny is ready," said Henry.

Benny got out of bed, washed his face, and dressed. A few minutes later Benny and Henry walked out the door of their cabin.

Henry and Benny walked along the path. As they walked, they passed the other small cabins under the trees. Each cabin had a small path that started at the front door. All of those smaller paths led to the wider path. And the wider path led to the main lodge.

Their grandfather had driven them to the Winding River Lodge after dinner the night before. For many years, Grandfather had been friends with the family that owned the lodge. It was just an hour away from Greenfield by car, but it was like another world. There was forest as far as the eye could see. People came from all over the state to enjoy the wonders of the outdoors and stay in the lodge's rustic cabins. Grandfather Alden had business to attend to back in Greenfield, so after they checked in, he had gone home. Soon after, the tired travelers had unpacked and gone to bed.

Violet was filming the light coming through the trees. Jessie stood beside her. "That will make a nice video," said Henry as they walked up to the girls.

"It's so pretty in the woods in the fall," said Violet.

"Breakfast is pretty, too," said Benny.

"Hold your horses, Benny," Jessie said with a laugh. "We're on our way to breakfast now." Jessie often acted motherly to Benny.

"Good morning," said a man as he walked past them on the path. He was carrying a painting easel in one hand and a folding chair in the other.

"Good morning," replied the Alden children.

"I hope he didn't eat all of the pancakes," said Benny after the man passed.

"It's early," said Jessie, "I'm sure there will be a few left for you."

The path to the main lodge twisted and turned through the woods as they walked. Violet turned the camera left and right, taking pictures. "This is such a beautiful place."

"Don't use up the memory card before breakfast," said Jessie.

"I won't," said Violet. "I can take pictures for two hours before it runs out of space."

"I hope it doesn't take us that long to get to breakfast," said Benny.

"It won't," said Henry. "Look." He pointed to the end of the path. There was the main lodge. Tall elms and colorful maple trees with red and yellow leaves surrounded it.

"Breakfast!" said Benny. He ran down the path and opened the door.

"Come right in," said a woman with curly silver hair. It was Maude Hansen, the owner of the Winding River Lodge. She was a longtime friend of Grandfather.

"Are you ready for breakfast?" said Maude. She rubbed her hands on her apron.

"Oh, yes," said Benny. "Do you have any pancakes left?"

"I saved some pancake batter just for you," said Maude. "Have a seat." She pointed at the dining room filled with tables.

Maude smiled as she stirred a bowl of batter with a spoon. Then she poured large circles of pancake batter on the griddle.

"Your breakfast will be ready in a few minutes," said Maude.

"Mrs. Hansen reminds me of Mrs. McGregor," said Jessie as she sat down at the table. Mrs. McGregor was Grandfather Alden's housekeeper. She had been taking care of the Alden children ever since they had come to live with their grandfather.

When their parents died, the Alden children ran away to live on their own. They feared they would be found and sent to live with their grandfather. They had never met him, and they worried he might be mean to them. So the children stayed in an old boxcar in the woods. The old railroad car quickly became their home, and they lived there until their grandfather found them. When the children saw how nice he was and how much he loved them, they went to live with him in Greenfield. Later, as a surprise, Grandfather had the boxcar moved into the backyard so they could play in it any time they liked.

The door to the main lodge opened, and a young woman with short brown hair walked in. She carried the newspaper under her arm. "Morning, Maude," she said.

"Good morning to you, Madison," said Maude.

"And good morning to all of you," said Madison. She walked up to the Aldens' table and sat down.

"Good morning," said the Aldens.

Madison took the newspaper out from under her arm and held it in front of her. Then she shook her head. "The nerve of that man!" she said to herself.

"What man?" asked Benny.

Madison turned the paper around to show

the Aldens. "Can you believe it?" she said. She pointed to a photo of man holding a golf club. "Donovan Golf Tournament to Go On," the headline said.

"Matthew Donovan is a wealthy business-man who stole millions of dollars from the company he works for," said Madison. "Then he disappeared into thin air. But his charity golf tournament is still going on. Unbelievable!"

Maude used a spatula to flip the pancakes over. "Now, Madison," she said. "I thought you were on vacation from the newspaper."

"I am, I am," said Madison. She put down the paper with a sigh.

"How can you be on vacation from a paper?" asked Benny.

"I'm a reporter," said Madison. "I write for this newspaper." She pointed to the words in large bold print at the top of the page: *Greenfield Gazette*.

"I'm the business reporter. And that Matthew Donovan is making me crazy. Where did he disappear to? What did he do with all of that money?"

"A bad penny always turns up," said
Maude. "In the meantime, you should enjoy
your vacation."

Maude used the spatula to move the
pancakes from the griddle to the plates.
Then she put the plates on the counter. "Your
pancakes are ready. Come and get them while
they're hot."

Madison and the Alden children stood up
and walked over to pick up their plates.

"You're right, Maude. I should enjoy my
vacation," said Madison. "Donovan is work
and this is my time off. I need something
new for my *Hauntings* blog. I'll look for your
zombie while I'm here."

"Zombie?" said Benny. His eyes opened
wide. "What is a zombie?" asked Benny.

"A creature from a scary movie," says
Jessie.

Maude shook her head as she carried the
maple syrup jug to the table. "Madison, you
know that old zombie legend isn't real. It's just
an old campfire story. My great grandfather

made it up to bring in the tourists. But I don't need any folks tromping through the woods looking for zombies."

Maude turned and looked at the Aldens. "What I need is some help clearing out the trail to the old fishing lodge. My grandson Jake and his friends won't be up until after lunchtime. I'd do it myself, but I want to make peach cobbler for lunch."

Benny almost jumped out of his chair. "Peach cobbler? I'll help clear the trail!"

The Alden children laughed.

"We'll all help," said Henry. He looked at Jessie and Violet. They both smiled.

"I can film our work," said Violet. She held up the new camera.

"It will be fun," said Jessie.

"Good," said Maude. "Now there will be no more talk about zombies." Maude looked over at Benny and then back at Madison.

"Okay," said Madison. "Just a nice, quiet vacation for me."

"Quiet?" said Benny. "It's not quiet here. I heard an owl hooting last night."

"We're in the woods, Benny," said Henry.

"And owls live in trees," said Jessie.

"Yes, we have lots of owls here at the Winding River Lodge," said Maude. She patted Benny on the head. "They won't hurt you."

"But it was hooting so loudly, it woke me up," said Benny.

"Owls hoot loudly when someone disturbs them," said Maude.

"Did the light in the woods bother them?" asked Benny.

"A light in the woods?" said Maude. "Where did you see that?"

"In the woods behind our cabin," said Benny.

"You can see the stars when it's dark," said Violet. "Was that what you saw, Benny?"

Benny shook his head. "No, it wasn't stars. It was a light moving in the trees."

"Like the flashlight we used to go to our cabin last night?" said Henry.

"Yes," said Benny, "but the light was on the other side of the cabin." He looked at

Maude. "Is that path too close to the owl's nest?"

Maude's eye opened wide. "There's only one path to the cabins. Behind the cabins it's just woods." Maude turned and walked back to the kitchen. "Not again," she whispered.

Henry looked at Jessie and Violet. What was going on?

Maude came back out of the kitchen carrying another plate piled high with pancakes. "You'll all need some more pancakes if you're going to clear the trail for me this morning."

Benny blinked. "More pancakes? I can always eat more pancakes."

CHAPTER 2

Helping Out

After breakfast, the Aldens followed
Maude out of the main lodge. They walked
around to the back of the building. "Here
is our toolshed," said Maude. She opened
a small wooden door, and they all walked
inside. The room was filled with tools.
There were shovels, rakes, wheelbarrows,
and more.

"Wow!" said Benny. "You have a lot of
tools."

Maude laughed. "We have a lot of trees!

14

We need all of these tools to keep them tidy."
She shook her head. "I used to have a work
crew come and help me every summer. But
business has been slow, so I couldn't hire
anyone this summer. And now that it's fall,
everything has grown even bigger."

"We can help you," said Henry.

"Yes," said Jessie. "We'll help you tidy up
the trail."

Maude smiled. "Your grandfather said you
were hard workers."

"What do we need to take with us?" asked
Henry. He was good with tools.

"You'll need a rake and some clipping
shears," said Maude. She lifted a pair of
clipping shears off their hook on the back
wall of the shed. She put the clipping shears
in a wheelbarrow. "We'll use the wheelbarrow
to carry the tools," said Maude.

"Let me help," said Henry. He took three
more clipping shears off the back wall and
put them in the wheelbarrow.

Benny pointed at a rake at the back of the
toolshed. "That rake is taller than I am," said

Benny. The Aldens laughed.

"That's why we use a wheelbarrow to carry all our tools," said Maude. "The wheel makes it easier to carry large loads." Maude looked at the Aldens again. "You'll need some work gloves, too." She opened a drawer in the workbench and took out four pairs. She gave a pair of gloves to each of the Alden children. "These will protect your hands," said Maude.

Benny put on his gloves. "Now I'm ready to work," he said.

Henry pushed the wheelbarrow out of the toolshed. "Which way do we go?" he asked.

"The trail on the right goes out to the old fishing lodge," said Maude. "Follow me."

Violet took the camera out of her pocket. "I'm going to film our adventure," she said.

Benny lifted his hands and waved at the camera.

"Now, act natural, Benny," said Violet.

"Natural?" said Benny.

"We're surrounded by nature," said Henry.

"I'm supposed act like a tree?" said Benny. He put his arms out like branches. The

Aldens laughed as they walked down the trail with Maude.

"These trees are beautiful," said Violet. She turned and looked at Maude. "Are you sad when the trees lose their leaves?" asked Violet.

"There is beauty in every season," said Maude. "After the leaves fall, the snow comes. The woods are quiet and peaceful then."

"That sounds wonderful," said Violet.

"But what about the zombie?" blurted Benny.

Maude turned and looked at Benny. "Now, don't you worry about that old story," said Maude. "It is just a scary story for the campfire. That's one of our traditions. We have a campfire at the old fire pit every night for our guests. We eat together and tell stories. The guests like it."

"So there isn't a zombie?" said Benny.

Maude shook her head. "No," said Maude. "There's not. Are you disappointed?"

"Not me," said Benny.

"Me neither," said Violet.

"Good," said Maude.

The Aldens followed Maude as she led them down the winding trail. When the trail narrowed, Maude stopped. The trees and bushes along the sides of the trail almost touched one another in the middle.

"Everything here needs to be cut back," said Maude. She lifted her hand and touched a low tree limb. "You'll need to cut both the bushes and the tree limbs."

"Jessie and I can cut back the trees," said Henry.

Violet put her hand on Benny's shoulders. "Benny and I will cut the bushes."

"This trail goes all the way out to the old fishing lodge," said Maude. She pointed in the other direction. "I like to keep it open all year, in case some of the guests want to use it."

Maude looked out at the forest for a moment. "You never know what could be creeping around in these woods," she said softly.

What was creeping around the woods? Violet waited for Maude to explain, but Maude didn't say anything more about it.

Maude walked over to the wheelbarrow. "It will take a few hours to clear the trail," she said. "Just push the cuttings off to the side."

"We can do that," said Jessie.

"Thank you," said Maude. "Your grandfather told me you were hard workers. I'll ring the bell when it's time for lunch."

"Lunch!" said Benny. "I don't want to miss lunch."

"I'll ring the bell extra loud for you, Benny," said Maude. She patted Benny's hair. "When you hear it, just put the tools in the wheelbarrow and come back to the main lodge."

"I will," said Benny.

"Okay, then," said Maude. "I'm off to make my peach cobbler."

"I can't wait," said Benny.

Maude waved and then turned and walked back to the main lodge.

Henry passed out the clipping shears and they all went to work. *Clip! Clip! Clip!*

"Are zombies real?" asked Benny.

"No," said Jessie, "they are not real."

"Then why is the reporter looking for one?" asked Benny.

"Some people like to talk about scary things," said Henry.

Benny stopped clipping branches. He wanted to be ready just in case something did happen. "What do the zombies look like in the movies?" asked Benny.

"Uh . . . They look like people walking around," said Jessie. She didn't want to upset Benny.

"That isn't scary," said Benny. He clipped a low branch.

"No, that's not the scary part," said Henry. He reached up and clipped a tree branch hanging over the trail. *Whump!* It fell to the ground. "What's scary about zombies is that they are dead."

"Wait a minute," said Benny. "How can they walk if they are dead?"

Henry stopped clipping and looked at Jessie. "We have to tell him."

"I don't want him to have nightmares," replied Jessie.

Benny looked at Jessie and Henry. "Nightmares about what?"

"The zombies in the movies," said Jessie.

"What do they do that is so scary?" asked Benny.

"They eat people," said Henry.

"They eat people?" said Benny. His eyes

opened wide. "That *is* scary!"

Jessie put her hand on Benny's arm. "It's just in the movies, Benny. Zombies aren't real."

"But this work is real," said Henry. "Benny, we need your help."

"You can count on me," said Benny. He went back to cutting bushes. *Clip! Clip!*

The Aldens worked on the trail for the rest of the morning. Henry and Jessie cut the high branches while Violet and Benny cut the low ones. When the pile in the middle of the trail got too big, they pushed the cuttings off to the side.

"It looks like we're making a wall," said Benny.

Dong! Dong!

"There's the bell," said Benny. "It's time for lunch!"

The Aldens put their tools into the wheelbarrow, just like Maude had asked. Then they walked back down the winding trail to the lodge. The closer they came to the main lodge, the more people they saw.

"Look," said Benny. "Everyone is coming at the same time."

"They all want to eat lunch," said Henry.

"I hope they save some peach cobbler for me," said Benny. "I'm hungry."

"We all worked up an appetite," said Jessie. "But I'm sure Maude will save some peach cobbler for you."

When the Aldens walked into the main lodge, they saw three teenagers. They looked to be a couple of years older than Henry. There were two boys and a girl. A boy with short, curly black hair had his arm around a girl with a blond braid that reached all the way down to her waist. The other boy had long brown hair. He was sitting at the table with his eyes closed.

"Which one do you think is Maude's grandson?" asked Violet.

"The one with the curly hair," said Jessie. "It's just as curly as Maude's hair."

Madison was sitting with the teens. "You grew up here, Jake," said Madison to the boy with curly black hair.

"My great grandparents opened this lodge a long time ago," Jake said to Madison. "Our family has lived here ever since."

Jessie looked at Violet. "You were right, Violet," said Jessie.

"Let's go sit with them," said Violet.

"Good idea," said Henry. "We can meet someone near our own age."

The Aldens walked over and sat at the teens' table.

"Can you tell me more about the Legend of the Winding River Zombie?" Madison asked Jake. "I want to write about it on my blog."

"You have a blog?" asked the girl with the long braid.

"Yes, I do, Abby," said Madison. "It's called *Hauntings*."

Jake poked the boy with his eyes closed. "Do you hear that, Caleb?"

Caleb opened his eyes and took out an ear bud. "What?"

"Madison has a blog about haunted things," said Jake.

"Whoa," said Caleb.

"What do you write about?" asked Abby.

"Oh, I have stories about haunted places all over New England," said Madison. "I'd love to add your zombie story."

"Our zombie?" said Jake.

"Whoa," said Caleb again.

Abby sat up and smiled. "We'll be famous!" She hugged Jake.

"That's the plan," said Jake.

"Can you tell me your zombie story?" said Madison.

"Sure," said Jake. "We want everyone to know about our zombie." Jake looked around the room to see who was listening. Most of the guests at the tables nearby were watching him. Henry, Jessie, and Violet moved in closer to hear the story. Benny stayed where he was. He wasn't sure he wanted to hear such a scary story.

"It's an old story, really," said Jake. "I've heard it all my life."

Violet took the camera out of her pocket and started filming.

"Well," said Jake. "As the story goes . . .

one day a body was found in the forest by the river."

Maude came out of the kitchen. "Jake," said Maude. "Don't tell campfire stories now. It's only lunchtime."

"Awww," said the guests.

Violet turned her camera off.

"I'll tell you tonight," said Jake, "at the campfire."

"I hope so," said Madison as she stood up. "I want to hear all about it."

Benny looked at Violet. "Is it true?" he asked. "Is there really a zombie?"

"I don't know," said Violet. She looked over at Jake. "I hope not."

CHAPTER 3

Working Together

After a hearty lunch and two helpings of peach cobbler, Benny was nice and full. "Now I'm ready to go to work," said Benny.

"That's wonderful, Benny," said Maude. She walked around the table and put her hand on Jake's head. Jake turned around and looked up at his grandmother.

"Jake," said Maude. "I want you to go and help the Aldens with the trail."

"Okay, Grandma," said Jake. "I'll help."

Maude looked at Abby and Caleb. "You

27

can help, too," said Maude.

"We'd love to help," said Abby. She put her long braid over her shoulder and stood up.

Caleb didn't say anything. He was listening to his music. His ear buds were in and his eyes were closed. His long brown hair swung from side to side as he moved his hands up and down and pretended to play the drums.

"Caleb!" said Maude.

Jake put his hand on Caleb's shoulder. Caleb stopped drumming and opened his eyes. "He'll help out," said Jake.

Caleb looked at Jake and then at Maude. He nodded his head.

"Good," said Maude. She looked at Jake. "You know where the tools are."

"We're on our way," said Jake.

The Aldens went with Jake and his friends to the toolshed.

"We already took some of the tools out on the trail earlier," said Henry.

"That's okay," said Jake. "Grandma has lots of tools. She used to have a big work crew come up every summer. Now we do it all ourselves."

Jake picked up three clipping shears and three rakes and put them into a wheelbarrow. Then he picked up the wheelbarrow handles and pushed it out of the toolshed.

Violet took the camera out of her pocket as they all walked along the trail. "It must be so nice to live here all year," she said.

Jake looked at Violet. "That's a small camera," he said. "Can I try it?" He put the wheelbarrow handles down.

"Sure," said Violet. She handed the camera to Jake.

Jake looked at the camera carefully. "How long can you film on this?"

"It records for two hours," said Violet.

"That's a long time for such a small camera," said Jake. He gave the camera back to Violet. Then he picked up the wheelbarrow by the handles and pushed it down the trail.

"Here we are," said Benny when he saw the wheelbarrow the Aldens had left on the trail.

"We started after breakfast," said Henry.

"I can see that," said Jake.

"I was asleep," said Caleb.

"You always sleep through breakfast," said Abby.

"Musicians don't do mornings," said Caleb. He closed his eyes and moved his hands as if he were playing the drums.

Jake looked at the trail. "You've done a lot of work so far," he said. "This won't take long."

With everyone working together, they cleared the brush along the trail very quickly. Henry and the teens trimmed the tall branches. Jessie, Violet, and Benny did the lower ones. And everyone helped move the brush to the edges of the trail.

"The trail is much wider now," said Benny.

"That's what Grandma wants," said Jake. "Then anyone can go to the old fishing lodge." He pointed to a small cabin by the river. "She likes to keep it open in case someone wants to use it."

"Is anyone staying there now?" asked Jessie.

"No," said Jake. "We don't use it as a guest cabin anymore. We just keep it open in case the weather gets bad and someone who is fishing needs shelter."

"How is the fishing out here?" asked Henry.

"Pretty good," said Jake. "Every day, Grandma asks someone to catch our dinner."

"Talking about dinner is making me hungry," said Benny. "Can we go have a snack?"

"Let's put the tools away first," said Jessie. "Then we can ask Maude."

"Grandma's kitchen is always open," said Jake.

"That's my kind of kitchen," said Benny. He picked up his rake and put it in Henry's wheelbarrow. Jake and Henry pushed the two wheelbarrows back to the toolshed. After everyone put their tools away, they all went into the kitchen.

"We're home," blurted out Benny.

"Now sit down and have something to eat, Benny," said Maude. "I know you must be hungry after all that work."

"I am," said Benny. "I am."

Everyone laughed.

Maude put a basket of apples and a bowl of cheese slices on the table. Benny walked up to the table.

"Wash up first," said Maude. "Then you can eat."

"Yes, ma'am," said Benny. He walked over and stood in line at the sink.

"Jake," said Maude. "Can you take the Aldens to a good fishing spot after you eat? It's their turn to catch our dinner."

"That will be fun," said Jessie.

"How many fish do we need to catch?" asked Henry.

"We'll eat whatever you catch at dinner tonight," said Maude. "But don't worry. We'll be serving other food as well."

"I'll catch a big fish for you," said Benny. He held his hands out to show how big it would be.

Maude smiled. "That sounds great, Benny. Are you sure that will be big enough for you to eat?"

Benny looked at his outstretched arms. "I think so," he said.

"Oh, Benny," said Violet.

After everyone ate their snacks, Jake took the Aldens back to the toolshed behind the main lodge. He opened a tall cabinet. "All of the fishing gear is in here," said Jake.

Benny walked up and looked inside the cabinet. He saw a small fishing rod. "This one is just my size," he said.

Jake handed Benny the short fishing rod. "Then it's yours," said Jake. "I used the same rod when I was your age."

"Did you catch a lot of fish?" asked Benny.

Jake smiled. "Of course!"

"I thought so," said Benny. He put the fishing rod over his shoulder.

Jake looked at Violet. "I have one for you, too," he said. He gave Violet a medium-sized rod.

Then Jake looked at Henry and Jessie. "You can both use taller rods." He gave them each a tall fishing rod. "Now I'll take you to a good fishing spot."

"Good," said Benny. "I want to catch a lot of fish."

"We have a lot of people to feed," said Henry.

"We'll do our best," said Jessie.

"Maude said that whatever we catch is fine," replied Violet.

Jake picked up a tackle box and a big plastic bucket. "Follow me," said Jake. The Aldens followed Jake out of the toolshed. Jake led them back down the winding trail they had just cleared.

"It's a lot easier to walk this way now," said Jessie.

"It's still pretty," said Violet. She took the camera out of her pocket and started filming.

Jake walked past the old fishing lodge and stopped at the edge of the river. "Here we are," said Jake. "It's my lucky spot."

"Why is it lucky?" asked Benny.

Jake pointed at the cabin behind them. "That's the first place our zombie was seen," said Jake.

"Your zombie?" said Benny.

"The Winding River Zombie," said Jake. He patted Benny on the shoulder. "I've always had good luck fishing here, and you will, too."

"You said that was just an old family story," said Henry.

"It is," said Jake. He looked at the woods and smiled.

"Have *you* seen the zombie?" asked Jessie.

"Well, uh, yes," stammered Jake.

"You have?" said Benny. "What did it look like?"

Jake shrugged his shoulders. "Oh, you know. It walked like this." Jake put his arms out and slowly lurched forward. Then he turned to leave. "I have to go help Grandma now."

The children watched as Jake walked back down the trail.

CHAPTER 4

Zombie Luck

"Will we see the zombie, too?" asked Benny.

"Jake said it's just an old story," said Jessie.

"But he said he saw it," said Violet.

"I've seen zombies in the movies, too," said Henry, "but they're not real."

Henry put his hand on Benny's shoulder. "It's a good story for the tourists, Benny," said Henry. "Nothing more." He pointed at the old cabin behind them. "They call it the old fishing lodge, not the old zombie lodge."

Benny looked at the cabin. Then he turned and looked at the river. The sun was shining down on the river as it flowed past. The birds were singing. Everything was calm and peaceful.

Henry knelt down and opened the tackle box. The lures were in the small, open drawers at the top. Some lures looked like small, shiny metal fish. Some had feathers and beads with long hooks that pointed in three directions at once.

"What kind of lure do you want to use, Benny?" asked Henry.

Benny looked at the shiny-fish lures and the lures with the feathers and beads. Then he saw the long plastic worms.

"Fish love worms," said Benny. "But which color is better? Do I want red or blue or black?" Benny looked at the plastic worms in the tackle box again. What would a fish like?

"I want this one," said Benny. He took a long, red plastic worm out of the tackle box. "It looks like a real worm."

Benny put the fishing line through the

loop at the end of the worm lure. Then he tied a knot. "Now what?" asked Benny.

"Cast your line into the water," said Henry, "like this." Henry flicked his wrist and the end of the fishing line flew back over his shoulder. Then Henry moved his arm toward the river and the end of the fishing line flew over his head and dropped into the water. Benny watched as the red-and-white bob on Henry's line floated on the surface.

"I can do that," said Benny. He flicked his wrist back and the fishing lines flew back over his shoulder. Then he moved his arm forward and the line flew over his head and into the river. His red-and-white bob floated on the water next to Henry's.

Jessie cast her line into the water and so did Violet. Benny watched their lines bob up and down in the water.

"Come on, fish," said Benny.

Crack!

Benny turned around. What was that?

The sound came from behind the old fishing lodge. Was someone there?

Benny squinted his eyes. He could see something in the forest behind the cabin. And that something was moving!

Benny leaned in closer to take a better look. Then a man came out from behind the trees.

Benny watched as the man lurched across the clearing. Why was the man moving like that? And why were his clothes torn?

Benny gasped! Could it be the zombie?

Benny grabbed Jessie's sleeve and pulled on it. "Look!" said Benny. Then he turned and pulled Henry's sleeve. "There it is!"

"What is it?" asked Jessie.

"It's the zombie," said Benny. "Over there!"

Benny pointed at the trees behind the fishing lodge. But the figure was gone.

"I don't see anything," said Jessie.

"Neither do I," said Henry.

Violet gave the camera to Henry. "Can you see it with this?"

Henry pressed the button on the camera so he could see up close. "It's just trees," said Henry. He gave the camera back to Violet.

She put it in her pocket.

Benny put his fishing pole down. "But I saw a zombie," said Benny. "He was right behind the old fishing cabin."

"Benny," said Jessie. She put her hand on Benny's shoulder. "Even in the movies, zombies don't come out in the daytime."

"It must've been something else," said Henry.

Benny looked at the woods again. "Who was it?"

"It was probably Jake," said Jessie.

"Maybe that's how they keep the zombie legend alive," said Henry.

"By pretending to be the zombie?" said Violet.

"Maybe," said Henry.

"How will a zombie give me good luck when I fish?" asked Benny.

Henry laughed. "That's an old story, too."

"An old *fishing* story," said Violet.

"Fishermen love to tell stories about the fish they catch, Benny," said Jessie. "But that doesn't mean the stories are true."

"Oh," said Benny. He picked up his fishing rod. A moment later, his line was back in the water.

Benny looked back at the woods one more time. Zombies weren't supposed to come out in the daytime. That's what Jessie said. But what if the zombie didn't know that?

Benny felt a tug. He turned around. It was his line.

"Henry," said Benny. "It's a fish!"

"Reel it in slowly," said Henry.

Benny turned the handle on his reel. Then there was another tug on the pole. Benny turned the handle on the reel again. The pole bent down as the fish tried to pull away. "It's a big one," said Benny.

"Keep reeling it in," said Henry.

Benny turned the handle on the reel again. It was getting harder and harder to make it turn.

Splash! The fish came up out of the water.

"You caught it," said Jessie.

Violet took the camera out of her pocket and turned it on. "Wait until Grandfather sees this."

"I caught a fish, Grandfather," Benny said to the camera.

"He will be so proud," said Jessie.

The Aldens fished the rest of the afternoon. Henry caught two fish and Jessie and Violet each caught one.

"Five fish," said Henry. "Pretty good for one afternoon."

"Let's bring these fish back to Maude," said Jessie. "She can cook them for dinner."

"Dinner!" said Benny. "I can carry them." He tried to lift the bucket. It barely budged.

"The bucket is heavy now," said Violet. "It's full of fish."

"Can you carry my fishing rod, Benny?" asked Henry.

"Sure," said Benny. He put the bucket handle down and picked up Henry's fishing rod instead. Henry picked up the bucket. The Aldens walked back down the trail to the main lodge.

"We're back!" said Benny as he opened the door.

"What have we here?" said Maude.

"Five fish," said Benny.

"Jake took us to a great spot," said Henry.

"By the old fishing lodge," said Violet.

"That's the best spot on the river to catch fish," said Maude. "Let's take these fish into the kitchen and get them ready."

Henry carried the bucket with the fish into the kitchen. "Put the bucket in the big sink," said Maude.

"Sure," said Henry. He lifted up the bucket and put it into the deep sink. Maude put on her apron. Then she washed her hands.

Violet took her camera out of her pocket and started filming. "What happens next?"

"I'll get the fish ready to eat," said Maude.

"I can hardly wait," said Benny.

"Benny," said Maude. "Can you put the fishing poles away?"

"Yes, I can do that," said Benny. He took the other two fishing poles from Violet and Jessie. Now he had all four.

Violet took a picture of Benny holding all four fishing poles. "Grandfather will like that," she said.

"Do you need help?" asked Jessie.

"No," said Benny. "I can carry all of them by myself." Benny put two poles over each shoulder.

"Let me get the door for you," said Jessie. She walked over and held the kitchen door open.

"Thanks," said Benny. He walked out the kitchen door. Then he walked around to the back of the lodge to the toolshed. Benny tugged on the toolshed door with his toe. The door swung open. Benny walked into the shed and over to the fishing cabinet. He used his toe to open the cabinet, too. Then he heard voices outside the toolshed.

"And when it gets close to you . . ." Benny heard Jake's voice say.

" . . . I scream," said Abby.

Benny froze. What were they talking about?

"Then I stop," said Caleb.

"Just for a minute, though," said Jake. "I want to zoom the camera in on your face."

"Should I grimace?" asked Caleb.

"I don't know," said Jake. "Let's try and see."

What is a grimace? wondered Benny. *Does it have something to do with the zombie?*

Then the voices moved away. Benny put the fishing poles into the cabinet and closed it. Then he opened the toolshed door and came out. The teens were gone.

Benny walked back to the kitchen. He had to tell Henry, Violet, and Jessie right away!

CHAPTER 5

The Zombie Legend

Benny opened the kitchen door and walked in.

"There you are, Benny," said Maude. "That was perfect timing." She handed Benny a big bag of marshmallows.

"Can you carry these out to the campfire?" said Maude.

"Are these for s'mores?" asked Benny. Benny loved hot and gooey s'mores. He forgot all about the teens and their grimace.

"Yes, they are," said Maude. "What is a

campfire without s'mores?"

"Yum," said Benny.

"Here we go," said Maude. Henry carried the fish, Jessie carried the corn, and Violet carried the chocolate bars and the graham crackers. They all walked down the trail to the fire pit.

"You can put it right here on the picnic tables," said Maude. The Aldens set all of the food down. There was already a big bowl of coleslaw and a platter of rolls on the table with the red-and-white checkered tablecloth. An ice cooler filled with drinks sat next to the table with the blue-and-white checkered tablecloth.

Maude picked up the long tongs and walked over the fire pit. The fire was already burning, and there were two-dozen foil-wrapped packages on top of the coals.

"What are you making?" asked Violet.

"Fire-baked potatoes," said Maude as she turned the foil wrapped potatoes over. "They have to cook for over an hour, so I put them in a while ago."

"It takes a lot of planning to cook outdoors," said Jessie.

"Yes, it does," said Maude. "But everything tastes better when you cook it outdoors. And the guests really like it. So we eat outside as long as the weather permits." She used tongs to put the foil-wrapped corn and fish into the fire. "Dinner will be ready soon."

More and more lodge guests came down the trail to the fire pit. It looked as if everyone staying at the lodge had come out for dinner.

"They really do like to eat outside," said Henry.

"The view is much better outside," said Violet. She took the camera out of her pocket and filmed the people around the fire pit.

"But what about the zombie?" asked Benny.

"That was probably Jake," said Henry.

Violet turned off her camera. "We don't know for sure," said Violet.

"So we won't say anything," said Jessie. "Okay, Benny?"

"Okay," said Benny.

A few minutes later, dinner was ready.

Maude used her long tongs and took all of the foil-wrapped food out of the fire. She put all of the food on big platters. As she unwrapped the foil, a wondrous smell filled the air.

Benny stood up and walked to the end of the table. He picked up a plate.

"I think someone is hungry," said Jessie.

"Benny is always hungry," said Violet.

Henry came up and stood behind them. "Yes, he is, but this food really does smell delicious."

"We have to see how our fish tastes," said Benny.

"You'll know in a minute," said Maude. She put a serving of fish on Benny's plate.

"Thanks," said Benny. He walked over and sat by the campfire. Violet, Jessie, and Henry joined him.

"Now I can eat our fish," said Benny. He used his fork to take a big bite. "Mmm!"

Henry took a bite of fish, too. "It's very tasty."

"Everything tastes better when you eat outdoors," said Violet.

Jessie took a bite. "And the fish is fresh, too. We just caught it this afternoon."

"Right after I saw the zombie," said Benny. "Maybe it was good luck."

Jessie gave Benny a quick look.

"I won't tell anyone," said Benny. "I promised."

After the guests were served, Jake filled up his plate and came over to sit with the Aldens. "I see you had good luck with the fish," said Jake.

"Yes, we did," said Henry. "It was a good fishing spot."

"I told you the zombie was good luck," said Jake.

It was hard for Benny to stay quiet. "I saw . . ." said Benny.

Jessie touched Benny's arm, and he stopped talking. All of the Aldens looked at Jake. What would he say?

"Jake," said Maude. "Can you help me?"

"Coming, Grandma," said Jake. He stood up and took his plate back to the table.

"That was close," said Violet.

"Sorry," said Benny.

"After we eat, we can help Maude clean up, too," said Henry.

"That's a good idea," said Jessie.

After the Aldens finished eating, they brought their plates back to Maude. "Where do these go?" asked Jessie.

"The dirty plates go over there," said Maude. She pointed at a bucket by the end of the table.

"I see it," said Violet.

The Aldens walked over and put their plates into the bucket.

"Do you want us to collect plates from the other guests?" said Henry.

"That would be wonderful," said Maude. "And I have a special task for you, Benny."

"For me?" said Benny. "What do you want me to do?"

Maude pointed at the bag of marshmallows he had carried out earlier. "Can you hand these out to our guests?"

"Sure," said Benny. He took the bag of marshmallows off the table. Then he walked around the campfire and gave each person two marshmallows. Jake followed behind Benny, passing out sticks.

Benny put the half-empty bag of marshmallows back on the table. Then he sat down and put his own two marshmallows on a stick. He leaned forward and held the marshmallows over the fire.

"Don't leave your marshmallows on the fire for too long," said Jessie.

"Or they will burn," said Violet.

"Or fall into the fire," said Henry. "Then you'll have nothing to eat!"

"Oh no! I don't want that to happen," said Benny. He pulled his stick out of the fire and put the hot marshmallows on top of the chocolate bar and the bottom graham cracker. After he put the top graham cracker on, he held the s'more tight and pulled out the stick. Mmm . . . now it was time to eat!

Benny took a bite. The outside of the marshmallow was toasted just a bit, but the inside was soft and sticky. S'mores were so good!

"Does anyone have a campfire story?" asked Maude.

"Tell us about the Winding River Zombie," said Madison. She was sitting on the other side of the fire pit.

Jessie looked at Henry. Now they would find out the story behind the zombie legend. Maybe that would help them figure out who had been walking in the woods this afternoon.

Jake looked over at his grandmother Maude. Maude nodded her head. "Go ahead," she said. "You know the story."

Jake leaned in toward the fire. He rubbed his hands together as he looked at the guests gathered around the fire.

Violet turned her camera to *record* as Jake began the story . . .

"A long time ago, a dead body was found in the forest by the river. It was here in our woods."

Jake waved his hand at the trees, and the guests at the campfire looked around at the woods.

Benny grabbed Jessie's hand.

"Don't be scared," whispered Jessie. "It's just a story."

"Go on," said Madison.

Jake continued. "It was the old hermit who lived in the woods. A hermit is someone who doesn't like to be around people. Great Grandpa said the man had lived in the forest for years."

"How sad," said Violet.

"My great grandparents called the sheriff," said Jake, "but he couldn't find the hermit's family. No one knew where he came from. So they buried him here in the cemetery by the Winding River."

Jake pointed toward the river, and everyone looked in that direction.

"Great Grandpa, Great Grandma, and the sheriff were the only ones that came to the service," said Jake. "But the next day, something strange happened."

"Uh-oh," said Benny.

Henry looked at Benny.

"Someone camping along the river said that he saw a stranger walk by his campground right before sunrise," said Jake. Then Jake stood up and moved his body as if he were walking. But Jake wasn't walking normally. He was lurching forward, just like he had done earlier at the river.

Benny whispered to Jessie. "Just like the zombie!"

Jessie nodded her head, but she also put her finger to her lips.

Benny nodded back. He would keep the secret.

"The camper walked up to the stranger and tried to help the poor soul," said Jake. "But when the camper reached out his arm, the stranger grabbed him. Then the stranger tried to bite the camper's arm with his bloody teeth!"

Jake pretended to bite his own arm.

Violet leaned over to Benny. "Is that what the zombie you saw did?" she whispered.

Benny shook his head. The zombie hadn't tried to bite anything.

Jake put his palms up and made a pushing motion. "So the camper pushed the stranger over and ran away. He jumped on his horse and left the campground. He left all of his things by the river. His food, his bed roll, his fishing pole, everything . . .”

Jake paused for a minute. Then he lowered his voice and continued . . .

“When the camper came back later with the sheriff, everything at his campsite was still there. It was just as he left it. The stranger wasn't hungry for food. But what did he want? Why did he try to bite the camper? They just didn't know.”

Jake shrugged his shoulders. So did Jessie. Biting a stranger *was* a strange thing to do. It didn't make any sense.

“Later that day,” said Jake, “the caretaker at the cemetery called the sheriff. Someone— or something—had been digging in the graveyard, and the old hermit's grave was dug up. The dirt that had covered the coffin was scattered all over the graveyard.”

Jake lowered his voice even more. Everyone had to lean in closer to hear him.

“Inside the grave, the coffin lid was pushed

away . . ."

Jake paused and looked at the guests sitting around the campfire.

"What a scoop that would be for my blog!" Madison interrupted. "Maybe even the *Gazette*!"

Jake quickly looked over at Maude, who was frowning.

Jessie looked at Maude, too. Why was she upset? Then Jessie remembered that Maude didn't like to talk about the zombie. And she didn't want visitors to come looking for it either.

Jake looked back at Madison and continued his story. "The coffin was empty," he said. "The dead man's body was gone! That's when they knew that the man they buried had become a zombie."

Suddenly there was a loud *CRACK* in the woods. Everyone turned to see what had made the sound.

Henry picked up a flashlight and shone it into the woods. Benny stood behind him. Violet grabbed Jessie's hand. The noises stopped.

"That was dramatic, wasn't it?" said Maude. "Who knew that our wildlife had such great timing?"

Some of the guests around the fire pit laughed.

Henry turned and looked carefully at Maude. She looked a bit nervous herself, but she was trying to calm her guests. Henry turned off the flashlight.

"The campfire is almost out," said Maude. "Jake, can you help me put it out all the way?"

Jake picked up a bucket by the fire pit and tossed sand on the fire. The fire hissed as it went out.

Benny stood up and looked at the woods. Now it was very dark. "Can you turn on the flashlight again, Henry?" said Benny.

"Sure," said Henry. He flipped the flashlight switch.

Jake walked over to the other side of the fire pit and picked up a rake.

"Will he use that to fight the zombie?" Benny whispered to Henry.

"Benny, you know zombies aren't real," said Henry. "Maude said it was just an animal in the woods."

"Yes, that's probably what it was," said Jessie.

"I hope so," said Violet. "That was a pretty scary story."

"Yes, it was," said Benny.

Jake walked around the fire pit and smoothed out the ashes. He poured more sand over the ashes that were still smoldering.

Maude stood up. "Time for bed, everyone."

"Let us help you clean up," said Henry. The Aldens picked up the containers they had carried to the fire pit. Jake and the teens helped carry the platters and the dishes back to the lodge kitchen.

"Thank you," said Maude. "Just leave them on the counter. I'll wash the dishes while I listen to my music." She turned on the radio by the sink. It was playing golden oldies music.

"Good night," said Maude. "Thank you for all of your help. I'll see you in the morning."

"Good night," said the teens.

"Good night," said the Aldens.

Benny could hear Maude singing as they walked down the path. After they passed the first few cabins, the singing faded away. Benny looked nervously at the woods. But nothing else happened.

When they reached their cabin door, Henry opened it. Benny stood at the door and turned around. He took the flashlight from Henry and shone it at the woods.

"Do you see anything?" asked Violet.

"No," said Benny.

"It was probably just a raccoon," said Jessie.

"Or a possum," said Henry. "There are lots of animals that hunt in the woods at night."

Benny went inside the cabin and closed the door. "That's what I'm afraid of," said Benny.

"It's like Maude said," said Henry. "It was the timing that made it so dramatic."

"It was very dramatic timing," said Violet. "Do you think Jake made the noise?"

"It couldn't have been Jake," said Jessie. "Jake was the one telling the story."

"What about the other teens?" said Henry.

"They weren't there tonight," said Violet.

"Do you think Caleb and Abby were in the woods?" asked Henry.

"Caleb," said Benny. "That reminds me. What is a grimace?"

"A grimace is the look on someone's face when they are in pain," said Jessie. "Like this." She closed her eyes partway and scrunched up her nose as if she had smelled something bad.

"Where did you hear that word?" asked Henry.

"When I was putting away the fishing pole," said Benny. "Caleb asked if he should make a grimace."

Violet shook her head. "That doesn't sound good."

"Do you think they were talking about the zombie?" asked Benny.

"We'll have to watch all three of them carefully tomorrow," said Jessie.

"Good idea," said Henry. "Now I'm ready for bed."

Henry, Jessie, and Violet washed up and went to bed.

Benny washed up and put on his pajamas. He lay on the bed, but he couldn't fall asleep. He couldn't stop thinking about the zombie.

What if his brother and sisters were wrong? What if there really was a zombie?

Benny heard the owl hoot. Then a light flashed in the window. What was that? Benny sat up in bed. Something was out there in the woods.

Benny looked around the room. Henry, Violet, and Jessie were fast asleep. How could he let them know something was out there in the woods without waking them? He had to show them some proof.

Wait a minute! Where was Violet's camera?

Benny looked at the nightstand by Violet's bed. The camera was next to the clock.

Benny walked over to the clock. It was ten o'clock. Benny picked up the camera and turned it on. He filmed the clock and then he walked over to the window.

Out in the woods, he saw a light flashing.

The owl hooted again.

What was out there?

Benny filmed the light as it moved away from the cabin. The light moved farther and farther away . . . until it disappeared.

Benny turned off the camera and put it back on Violet's nightstand.

"I'll show everyone in the morning," whispered Benny.

He went back to bed. The zombie was gone, for now. At last, Benny could relax. He pulled the covers to his chin and went to sleep.

CHAPTER 6

Zombie Clues

The next morning, Jessie stood over Benny. "Wake up, Benny," said Jessie.

"It's time for breakfast," said Violet

Benny opened his eyes. "Violet," said Benny. "I used your camera last night."

"That's okay," said Violet. "Grandfather said it was for everyone."

"I used it to take a video of the zombie," said Benny.

"The zombie?" said Henry.

"Oh," said Violet. She looked at the

camera but she didn't pick it up. She wasn't sure she liked having pictures of a zombie in her camera. It was a bit creepy.

Benny jumped out of bed. He picked up the camera from the nightstand. "It's right here," he said.

Benny turned on the camera. He went back to the video of the clock on the nightstand and pressed play. "Here it is."

Henry, Violet, and Jessie looked at the camera. They watched the light in the woods.

"See that," said Benny. "It's the zombie."

"Well . . ." said Henry.

"I don't see a zombie," said Violet.

"It's just a light," said Jessie.

"Then why was the owl hooting again?" said Benny.

"Someone was using a flashlight to go back to the cabin," said Henry.

"We used a flashlight last night, too," said Jessie.

"But Maude said there wasn't a trail to the cabins back there. And the owl didn't hoot at us," said Benny. "Something scared it."

"Let's look at it again," said Henry. He went back to the clock picture. Then he turned the sound up on the camera. "Okay, here we go . . ."

Henry pressed play. They heard the owl hooting. Then the video moved from the clock to the window.

Shuuursh! Shuuursh! Shuuursh! Shuuursh!

"What is that?" asked Benny.

"It doesn't sound like an animal," said Henry.

"What else could it be?' said Violet.

"It must be the zombie!" said Benny.

"But that's only a story," said Henry. "It's not real."

"Let's go out and look," said Jessie.

"We can film the evidence," said Violet, "even if it is scary . . ." Her voice trailed off.

"Don't worry, Violet. We'll be with you," said Jessie. She put her arm around Violet.

Violet closed her eyes. "Thanks."

After Benny got dressed, the Aldens walked out of the cabin.

"It went that way," said Benny. He pointed at the woods behind the cabin.

"Then let's go that way, too," said Henry.

"This is the way to the old fishing lodge," said Jessie.

"We worked on the trail here yesterday," said Violet.

"Look," said Benny. He pointed at the trail up ahead. Someone had pushed back the wall of branches they had cleared from the trail.

"Someone was here last night," said Benny.

"And they made a mess," said Violet. "That wasn't very nice. Someone could trip on these branches." The branches the children had neatly stacked on the side of the trail were scattered everywhere.

"What happened here?" said Jessie. She pointed at the ground. The dirt and grass were flattened. It looked as if something long and heavy had been dragged along the ground.

Benny looked at the flat area. It was as wide as a human body. "The zombie must have captured someone here," said Benny. "Then he dragged them away."

"Look at this," said Violet. There were clumps of uprooted grass and scuffs along the ground. "It looks like someone was kicking the ground. But why? What is going on?"

"Someone was fighting the zombie," said Benny. "They were trying to get away."

"There must be another explanation for this," said Henry.

"I hope so," said Violet. 'I don't want to see any zombies." She looked around nervously at the woods.

Benny bent down. He picked up a small piece of wood. It fit in the palm of his hand. "Look at this."

Benny showed the small wooden stake to Henry, Jessie, and Violet. The end was sharp and pointed, but the top was almost flat. It looked like a nail.

Violet filmed the small wooden stake in Benny's hand. Then she moved the camera to film the area behind Benny.

"I see two more," said Violet. "They're right behind you, Benny."

Benny turned around. He picked them up.

"The zombie must have come out of his coffin," said Benny.

"Do you think these are coffin nails?" asked Jessie.

Benny nodded his head. What else could they be?

"These look familiar, but I'm not sure what they are," said Henry. Then he put the three small wooden nails in his pocket. "We have to fix up the trail again," he said.

"Can we do it after breakfast?" said Benny. "I'm hungry."

"That's a good idea," said Jessie.

Henry patted the wooden nails in his pocket. "But don't tell anyone about this," he said. "We don't want Maude to worry. We'll come back and make it good as new after breakfast."

"*I'm* worried," said Violet. "What do you think is happening?"

"Someone was out in the woods at night," said Jessie.

"Maude mentioned that at breakfast yesterday," said Henry.

"She did?" said Benny.

"Not in so many words," said Jessie. "After

you told her about seeing the light, she said, 'Not again.' Then she went into the kitchen for a minute."

"But what does that mean?" asked Benny.

"Do you think someone is trying to scare the guests away?" asked Jessie.

"Maude did say that business has been slow," said Henry.

"But what does that have to do with a light in the woods?" said Henry. He tapped his pocket. "And these wooden nails?"

"It doesn't make any sense," said Violet.

"Do you think another lodge is trying to shut this one down?" asked Jessie.

"Maybe," said Henry. "But the Hansen family has lived here for years."

"And Maude is a nice person," said Benny.

"Yes, she is," said Violet. "That can't be it."

"Do you think it's the teens?" asked Jessie.

"Maybe," said Violet. "Caleb and Abby weren't by the fire pit when we heard the noise in the woods."

"And the sound I filmed was different," said Benny.

"Do you think that Madison is trying to make a big story for her blog?" asked Violet.

"She did say it was a big scoop," said Henry.

"And she wanted to put it in the paper, too," said Benny.

"We'll keep quiet about this until we know more," said Jessie. "Can you do that, Benny?"

"I won't tell anyone," said Benny. "I promise." He crossed his heart with his hand.

"Good," said Henry. "Let's go to breakfast."

The Aldens walked down the trail and into the main lodge. No one was there but Maude.

"Good morning," said Maude. "Are you ready for some pancakes?"

"Oh, yes," said Benny, "I have to eat a big breakfast so I can . . ."

Benny stopped and looked at Henry.

Henry shook his head.

"Can what?" said Maude as she poured the pancake batter on the griddle.

"Uh . . . so I can . . ." Benny stopped again.

Jessie leaned over and whispered in Benny's ear.

"So I can take a long walk on the trail," said Benny. He looked nervously at Maude, but Maude didn't look up.

"It's a fine day for a walk on the trail," said Maude. She turned over the pancakes. "I can walk for miles on a day like this."

Benny leaned over and whispered to Henry. "What if she sees the mess on the trail?"

Henry whispered back. "She has to make breakfast for everyone at the lodge first. We can fix it up while she is busy cooking."

"We'll have to work fast," said Benny.

"We will," said Henry.

Maude put the pancakes onto four plates. Then she turned and put the plates on the counter. "Come and get it!"

"Thanks!" said Benny. He walked over and picked up his plate.

Two plates of pancakes later, Benny was back in the toolshed behind the lodge. Henry put the tools they needed into the wheelbarrow.

"Henry, why does she have two kinds of rakes?" asked Benny. Henry knew all about tools.

"These rakes with the long tines are for raking leaves," said Henry. "We'll use those to move the leaves off the trail."

Benny followed as Henry pushed the wheelbarrow out of the toolshed. "But what about the other rakes?"

"These are garden rakes," said Henry. "They have short tines for moving dirt. We'll use them to smooth out the dirt on the trail."

Soon the Aldens reached the spot where the trail was torn up.

"Why did the zombie do this last night?" said Benny.

"I don't think a zombie did this," said Henry.

"But it happened at night this time," said Benny. "It must have been a zombie."

"I hope not," said Violet. "I don't want to see a zombie." She shivered.

"Lots of creatures come out at night in the woods," said Jessie. She moved a branch back to the edge of the trail.

Benny looked at the woods around him. "If it wasn't a zombie, then what was it?"

"Jessie's right," said Henry. "It could have been a squirrel or a raccoon or even a skunk."

"A skunk," said Benny. He held his nose. "I don't want to find a skunk!"

"Neither do I," said Violet. She waved her hand in front of her nose.

The Aldens looked at each other and then they started laughing.

"The woods are full of surprises," said Jessie.

"Let's get back to work," said Henry.

Henry, Jessie, and Violet carried more branches to the edge of the trail. Benny smoothed out the dirt.

Click! Click! Click! Violet heard something behind her. What was that? She quickly turned around. Oh. It was only the reporter and her camera. No need to worry.

"Did you think the zombie came out here last night?" said Madison. She snapped pictures of the torn-up ground.

Benny looked at Madison. How did she know he thought it was a zombie?

Benny looked Henry, but Henry shook his head. Benny remembered his promise. He didn't say a word.

"Look at how the grass and the dirt are flattened here," said Madison. "The zombie must have dragged a body here last night. I think this looks like the work of the Winding River Zombie," said Madison. "I was hoping to see it while I was here."

She walked to the edge of the trail and snapped another picture. "I must put this on my blog," said Madison. Then she turned and started walking back to the main lodge.

"I knew they would find it first," Madison said to herself as she walked away.

The Aldens waited until Madison was out of sight.

"Did you hear that?" asked Benny.

"Do you think Madison did this?" asked Violet. "Why would she?"

"So she has something to write on her blog," said Henry.

"And in the paper," said Jessie.

"Let's get to work," said Henry, "and clean this up before anyone else comes."

Jessie and Violet carried the rest of the branches to the edges of the trail. Then they raked the leaves and small branches over to the side.

When they were done, Benny put his rake into the wheelbarrow. Then he looked at the trail. "That looks much better."

"It certainly does," said Henry. "Now let's put our tools away."

Violet and Jessie put their rakes into the wheelbarrow. Henry pushed the wheelbarrow back to the toolshed and put the rakes away.

Dong! Dong!

"It's time for lunch!" said Benny.

The Aldens walked to the front of the lodge and went inside.

"There's Madison," said Jessie.

Madison was sitting at a table talking to some other guests. After the Aldens sat down, Madison stood up and came over. "Any more zombie sightings?" asked Madison.

"We didn't see any zombies," said Henry.

"If you see anything strange, be sure to let me know," said Madison.

"Okay," said Henry. He touched his pocket. The three small wooden nails were still in there.

"Thanks," said Madison and she walked back to the other table.

Henry leaned over and whispered, "Do you think Madison planted these little sticks so we would find them?"

"I don't know," replied Jessie. "Something strange is going on."

Violet nodded her head. Yes, it was all very strange and upsetting, too. What if Benny was right? What if there really was a zombie?

CHAPTER 7

Searching for Clues

After lunch, Maude came out of the kitchen and walked up to Madison. "It's your turn to catch our dinner, Madison," said Maude.

"But I don't know how to fish," said Madison.

Maude walked over to the table where the Aldens were sitting. Jake was sitting at the other end of the table with his friends Caleb and Abby. The teens were talking about zombies again.

"Can you help Madison catch our dinner?"

Maude asked Jake.

"Sure," said Jake. "We'll all help her fish." He looked at Abby and Caleb. Abby smiled and Caleb nodded.

"Thanks," said Maude. "Now I have to clean up lunch and get ready for dinner."

Maude went back into the kitchen and turned on her radio. Golden oldies music filled the room. Then Maude started singing.

Madison came over and sat at their table.

"I caught a fish yesterday," said Benny.

"You did?" said Madison. "I hope I can catch one, too."

"I'll take you fishing at the zombie's spot," said Jake. "I always catch a lot of fish there."

"The zombie's spot?" said Madison.

"The place where the zombie legend began," said Jake.

"Zombies rock," said Caleb. He moved his hands in a drumming motion.

Abby pretended to hold a microphone. "Zombies!" she sang out.

"Zombies?" said Madison. "Count me in." She reached into her bag and moved her hand around. "Wait a minute."

What is she looking for? Jessie wondered.

"I can't find my camera," said Madison. "I must have left it in my other bag." Madison pushed back her chair and stood up. "I want to take a picture of the place where the zombie legend began. I'll go and get my camera before we go fishing."

"Okay," said Jake. "We'll wait for you here."

"Good," said Madison. She quickly walked out of the lodge.

"What are *we* going to do after lunch?" asked Violet.

Henry patted his pocket. Then he put a finger up to his lips. Violet nodded her head.

"Oh, I get it," whispered Benny.

"Let's go back to our cabin," said Henry. "Then we can talk."

"Before we go back," said Jessie, "I want to stop in the gift shop. I promised Mrs. McGregor I would look for wind chimes."

"Wind chimes?' said Violet.

Jessie took an envelope out of her back pocket. "Mrs. McGregor says they sell wind chimes here. She wanted to give them to Grandfather for Christmas."

"So it's a secret," said Henry.

"We can keep a secret," said Benny.

"Of course we can," said Violet.

The small gift shop was at the front of the main lodge. While Jessie and Violet looked at the wind chimes, Henry and Benny walked around the store. Maybe there was a clue to the zombie legend here.

Then Benny saw the chocolate bars. They were right next to the cash register.

"Henry, do you have any money for snacks?" said Benny.

Henry laughed. "You just ate, Benny."

"I always have room for dessert," said Benny.

Henry looked at the sign under the candy. Then he reached into his pocket and took out some coins. "This should be enough," he said.

"Thanks," said Benny. He picked up the chocolate bar and handed it to the clerk behind the register.

While Benny paid for the chocolate bar, Henry looked at the wall next to the cash register. It was filled with magazines. Some had celebrities on the cover. Others were about the news. Then there were the sports magazines. On the cover of one, there was a man hitting a golf ball with a club.

"Wait a minute," said Henry. He took the small wooden nails out of his pocket. "I know what these are. They're golf tees."

By this time, Jessie and Violet had found the wind chimes that Mrs. McGregor wanted. They were standing behind Benny at the cash register.

"They're what?" asked Violet.

"They're golf tees," repeated Henry. He showed the golf tees to Violet and Jessie.

"Who plays golf in the woods?" asked Jessie.

"Lots of people do," said the clerk. "There's a big golf course just down the road."

"Do you sell these golf tees here?" asked Henry. He showed the clerk the three golf tees.

"No, we don't sell those here," said the clerk. "See the markings?" The clerk pointed at a small arrow on the side of the golf tee.

"I didn't notice that before," said Henry. He turned over the other two golf tees. They also had small arrows carved into them.

"That's a special brand," said the clerk. "They only sell those at the pro shops. They're too expensive for our customers. We only carry these." He pointed at a box on the shelf behind the counter.

"Do people play golf at the lodge?" asked Violet.

"No," said the clerk, "but some of our guests like to visit the golf course down the road during their stay. We keep these in stock just in case." He took the box off the shelf and put it on the counter.

"You know, there's big charity golf tournament going on this weekend. That's why we only have this one box of golf tees left. Did you want to buy it?"

"No, thanks," said Henry.

"Okay," said the clerk. "Here is your bag,

miss." He handed Jessie the bag with the wind chimes. "And your change."

Jessie put the change back in the envelope for Mrs. McGregor.

"Thank you," said Jessie.

"That was helpful," said Henry as they walked out of the shop.

"But what does it mean?' asked Violet.

"That zombies play golf," said Benny.

Henry laughed and then he said, "I've never seen *that* in the movies."

"The zombies in the movies are always chasing someone," said Jessie. She pretended to lurch like a zombie. "That's the only game they play."

"So zombies don't play golf," said Violet. "That's a relief."

"We'll find out who is really doing this," said Jessie. "Let's go back and look at the trail again."

"Good idea," said Henry.

"I have my camera ready," said Violet. She patted her pocket.

Benny led the way as they walked on the

trail out to the old fishing lodge.

"Slow down, Benny," said Henry. "We have to look for clues."

"What are we looking for?" said Benny.

"You'll know it when you see it," said Jessie.

The children could hear someone laughing. They followed the sound down the trail. Who could it be?

As they walked around the turn, they heard the laughter again. It was Madison. She was standing by the river with Jake, Caleb, and Abby. The Aldens moved behind a bush. They didn't want the teens to see them.

"It's hopeless," said Madison. "I just can't get the hang of this." Then she laughed again.

"I can help you," said Jake. He took the fishing pole from Madison and tied her lure to the end of the line.

"Here you go," said Jake. He handed the fishing pole to Madison.

"Thanks for your help," said Madison. "Though I doubt I will catch anything."

"Our zombie is good luck," said Jake. "We always catch fish out here."

Benny looked out at the river. Abby and Caleb already had their lines in the water.

Madison put her hand on Jake's shoulder. "That's good to hear," she said. Then she held up her fishing pole. "What do I do next?"

"Hold the pole in your hand like this," said Jake. He held his own fishing pole up. Then he flicked his wrist back and the line flew back over his shoulder.

"Okay," said Madison. She stood up and moved her pole just like Jake did.

Benny watched as the two fishing lines landed on the ground behind Jake and Madison. Wait a minute! Part of the grass and dirt by the river was flattened, too.

"Psst!" said Benny. He pointed at the flattened grass and dirt on the ground behind Madison.

Violet reached into her pocket and took out her camera. She zoomed in the camera and took a picture. *Click!*

"This looks like the other place," whispered

Violet. "The zombie must be real." She showed them the picture. The dirt and grass looked exactly the same.

Violet held the camera up and took another picture. *Click!*

Then she looked at the camera. "See these bushes?" said Violet. "They're all smashed down in one spot."

"Where?" whispered Henry.

Violet stood up and pointed at the bushes farther down the trail.

"The zombie starting dragging his victim over there," said Benny.

"Yes, it's just like the last time," said Jessie. "I wonder if there really is a zombie. No, that can't be right."

Henry stood up tall and looked over the bushes. "It goes from the trail all the way to the porch," whispered Henry.

"The zombie took the body in the old fishing lodge?" said Benny. "But no one lives there."

"Not so loud," said Henry. He pointed at Madison and the teens fishing by the river.

Henry turned and whispered to Violet. "Can you take some pictures of the trail?"

"Sure," said Violet. She leaned around the tree next to the bush where they were hiding. *Click! Click! Click!* Then she crouched back down.

Benny looked at the river again. No one was looking this way. He quickly walked to the next tall bush. Henry was right behind him.

Benny ran over to the trail. He looked left and right but saw nothing. So he walked around the next turn, and then he heard a crunch.

What was that? Benny stopped and lifted up his shoe. It was a golf tee. He turned it over. It had the small arrow on it. The zombie had been here!

Benny looked around. He saw another one! And another one . . .

Benny bent down to pick up three golf tees. They looked just like the other ones. Then Benny felt a tap on his shoulder. It was the zombie! Benny jumped up and started to run away.

"Benny!" whispered Henry. "It's only me."

Benny stopped. Then he turned and looked at Henry. Henry had taken the three golf tees out of his pocket. He was holding them in his right hand.

Benny walked over to Henry and held out his own right hand. The three wooden tees in Benny's hand looked just like the ones in Henry's hand. It was a perfect match.

CHAPTER 8

Fore!

Back at their cabin, the Aldens talked about their clues.

"What do we know so far?" asked Jessie.

"I saw a light in the woods at night," said Benny.

"Twice," said Violet. "It happened two nights in a row."

"And there was a strange sound, too," said Benny.

"Later, we found the expensive golf tees by flattened grass," said Henry.

"Twice," said Benny.

"And they're not from the lodge," said Violet.

"So someone brought the golf tees with them," said Henry.

"The grass and dirt was flattened all the way to the fishing lodge," said Jessie.

"But it wasn't flat everywhere," said Henry. "The flat part was only a foot or so wide. It wasn't done by a mower or anything like that." Henry knew his tools.

"Don't you think the zombie was dragging his victim back to the fishing lodge?" said Benny.

"I haven't heard about any victims," said Jessie.

"No one is missing," said Violet.

"So it's not a zombie," said Henry. "But what does all this have to do with the golf tees? It doesn't make sense."

"Maybe it's not supposed to make sense," said Jessie. "It is a legend after all."

"But why tell it?" asked Violet. "There must be something we're missing."

Benny's stomach grumbled. "I know what's missing," said Benny. "We're missing dinner."

"Okay, Benny," said Jessie. "Off to dinner we go."

* * *

After eating dinner and s'mores by the fire pit, Violet wiped off her fingers and took the camera out of her pocket. Grandfather would love to see this. Everyone was telling stories.

Violet filmed the other guests sitting by the fire pit. The man who had gone off to paint that first morning was telling his wife about a beautiful spot he had found by the river. *I'll have to go and see it for myself*, thought Violet.

The couple next to them had gone hiking on the trail that led all the way up to the waterfall. They were telling another guest all about it.

"And we saw them catch the fish we ate for dinner," said the man.

"Fresh is best," said the woman.

"I couldn't agree more," replied her companion.

Violet turned in a full circle around the campfire. It looked like everyone from last night had come back for another dinner outdoors.

Then she turned her camera toward Benny, Jessie, and Henry. They were sitting next to Jake, Caleb, and Abby. Caleb and Abby hadn't been at the fire pit last night.

Violet filmed Benny as he made another s'more.

"Are you getting this?" asked Benny.

"You're the star of the show," replied Violet.

"A food show," said Jessie.

"I like food," said Benny. He took a big, hot, gooey bite, and then he licked his lips. Benny really liked s'mores.

Violet turned her camera back to the teens. They were talking about zombies again.

"And then the zombie comes up behind her," said Jake.

Violet tapped Jessie on the shoulder and pointed to Jake. "Listen," she whispered.

"And she screams," said Caleb.

Jessie whispered Henry's ear. "Listen."

Henry quietly turned to listen.

"And she trips," said Jake. "She's so scared that she trips on a branch."

"That will hurt," said Abby.

"Yes, it will," said Jake. "But that doesn't stop the zombie."

Benny's eyes grew wide. He started to stand up, but Henry put his hand on Benny's shoulder. Benny stayed put.

"He's slowly moving closer," said Caleb, "step by stumbling step."

"So the girl looks up at the zombie and screams," said Abby.

"Yeah, that's right," said Jake.

"And then the zombie gets closer and closer," said Caleb.

"Until it's standing right over the girl," said Jake.

"Like this," said Caleb. He stood over Abby, his arms reaching down to grab her.

"And I move in for a closer shot," said Jake.

Abby leaned back and waved her arms as she pretended to scream. "So she screams even louder," said Abby.

"But no one hears her in the woods," said Jake.

"What next?" said Caleb.

"I'm not sure," said Jake.

The teens stood up and walked away from the campfire.

"Did you hear that?" said Benny. "Someone is going to get shot!"

"But not with a gun, Benny," said Violet.

"That's good," said Benny. He breathed a sigh of relief. Then he sat up straight. "Wait! How do . . ."

"With this," said Violet. She held up her camera. "Remember how Jake looked at my camera on the trail? He knows a lot about cameras."

"I get it," said Jessie. "A closer shot is a camera shot."

"Jake and his friends must be making a movie," said Henry.

"A movie?" said Benny.

"A zombie movie," said Henry. "Jake is filming Caleb chasing Abby."

"If Caleb is chasing Abby, then he must be the zombie," said Violet.

"But what about the light I saw?" asked Benny.

"Abby is probably using a flashlight so she won't trip in the dark," said Henry.

"So the zombie isn't real?" said Benny.

Jessie shook her head.

Benny breathed another sigh of relief. "That's good," said Benny. Then he sat up again. "But what about the golf tees?"

"We'll figure that out in the morning," said Henry.

"Okay," said Benny.

CHAPTER 9

A Zombie in the Woods

"I'm glad there's not a real zombie," said Benny as they walked back to their cabin after the campfire.

Crack! Something was moving in the woods.

Henry turned the flashlight toward the sound.

A man standing behind a tree raised his arm to cover his face. It was a zombie!

Benny grabbed Jessie's hand. What was the zombie going to do? The children waited

for the zombie to make a move.

The zombie moaned loudly. Then he turned and lurched away. He was pulling a body behind him!

Snap! Snap! Crack! The woods made noise as the zombie dragged the body behind him.

"Now what?" asked Jessie.

"Now we go back to the cabin," said Henry.

The children ran to the cabin. When they got inside, Henry locked the door.

"Do you believe in zombies now?" asked Benny.

"Well," said Henry. He wasn't so sure anymore. After all, he had seen it with his own eyes.

"There must be an explanation for this," said Henry.

"I hope so," said Violet.

"Did you get a picture of it?" asked Jessie.

"No," said Violet. "I was so surprised I forgot I had my camera."

"That's what we do next," said Henry. "We have to capture the zombie—"

Benny gasped.

"—on camera," finished Henry. "It didn't attack us. We'll be okay if we keep our distance."

"That's true," said Jessie. "It didn't come after us at all. It was like we surprised it . . . or something."

"*Or something* is right," said Violet.

"But we have to have proof before we say anything," said Henry.

Benny looked at the cabin window. "The owl hoots every night," said Benny.

"And when it does," said Henry, "we'll go out and capture the so-called zombie—on camera."

Violet held up the camera. "I can zoom the camera in from far away. Then we don't have to get close to the zombie." She shivered as she thought about the zombie.

"If we're going back out," said Benny, "then I'm not going to put on my pajamas. The zombie could run away while I'm getting dressed."

"That's a good idea, Benny," said Jessie. "We can go to bed with our clothes on."

Benny took off his shoes and put them right next to his bed. That way he could put them on as soon as he saw the lights in the woods.

After they all washed up, Henry turned out the lights. To anyone outside the cabin, it looked like the Aldens had gone to sleep.

Benny lay on his bed. He tossed and turned as he waited for the lights in the woods. He closed his eyes. Maybe he could sleep just a bit.

Hoot! Benny heard the owl outside his window. He sat up in bed. The light was flashing in the woods behind the cabin.

Henry jumped out of bed. Jessie and Violet sat up. They all put on their shoes. Henry grabbed the flashlight and Violet picked up the camera.

Henry opened the cabin door. "Here we go!"

The Aldens walked out of the cabin and into the night.

"The light is coming from that side," said Benny.

"I'll lead the way," said Henry. He walked into the woods. Benny, Jessie, and Violet followed him.

Up ahead, the light was flashing.

Crick! Crack! Someone was running in the woods.

Henry stopped and raised his hand. Everyone waited a minute.

"Do you hear that?" whispered Henry.

Benny nodded his head. "The light is over there," whispered Benny.

"We don't want to get too close," whispered Henry. "We don't want them to see us."

"I can't see it with my camera yet," said Violet.

"We'll have to move a little closer," said Henry.

Crick! Crack! There it was again. That noise in the woods.

Someone was running.

"Let's go," said Henry. They followed the sounds and the light.

When they got closer, Henry stopped again. "Violet, can you see anything?"

Violet lifted up her camera. "I see Jake," whispered Violet. "He's filming with a video camera."

"He's making a movie," said Jessie, "just like we thought."

"What else do you see?" asked Henry.

Violet moved her camera over. "I see Abby. She's holding a flashlight."

"That's the light I saw," said Benny. Then he thought a moment. "Wait a minute, where is the zombie?"

"Do you see Caleb?" asked Henry.

"He was pretending to be the zombie at the campfire," said Jessie.

"I don't see him," said Violet. She gave the camera to Henry.

Henry lifted up the camera and looked at the teens. He saw Jake and Abby and something else. It was someone dressed up as a zombie.

"Benny, I think we found your zombie," said Henry. "It *is* Caleb. Take a look."

Henry gave the camera to Benny.

"Caleb is the zombie?" said Benny. "Why was he trying to scare me?"

Benny looked into the camera. He saw Jake holding his movie camera. Then he saw Abby. She was crying and running away . . .

Benny moved the camera. She was running away from a zombie! The zombie was moving slowly, with his hands out in front of him. The zombie's long hair swayed back and forth as he walked.

"Wait a minute," said Benny. "That zombie has long hair!"

"Caleb has long hair," said Jessie.

"But the other zombie didn't have long hair," said Benny. "He had short hair. Remember?"

Jessie looked at the dark woods all around them. They had found a zombie in the woods, but it wasn't the right one. Who else was out there?

"Could it be true?" asked Jessie. "Is there really a Winding River Zombie?"

"I hope not," said Henry.

"Me too," said Violet.

CHAPTER 10

Unmasked!

After breakfast, the Aldens walked along the winding trail that went out to the old fishing lodge.

"There must be an explanation for this," said Henry.

"What is it?" asked Benny.

"We'll follow the clues and find out," said Jessie.

"I see Madison," said Violet. She pointed at the reporter. *Click! Click! Click!* Madison was taking pictures of the flattened dirt and grass next to the trail they had cleared earlier.

"Don't let her see us," said Henry.

The Aldens quickly stepped into the woods and hid behind a tree.

"The zombie came back," said Violet softly.

"The trail is torn up again?" whispered Henry.

"Yes, it is," said Violet. "Here, look for yourself." She gave the camera to Henry.

Benny looked over at the old fishing lodge. No one lived there, but something was different. What was it?

Benny closed his eyes and then he opened them again. It was the porch. There was something new on the porch. It was a tall, skinny bag filled with black-and-silver sticks. Each stick had a big silver handle at the top.

"What is that on the porch?" said Benny.

"It's a golf bag," said Henry. "See the golf clubs sticking out of it?" Then he put his hand on his forehead. "That's it!"

"What?" said Benny.

"Do you remember Matthew Donovan,

the guy that was making Madison crazy?" said Henry.

Jessie nodded her head. "The missing millionaire," she said.

"He was missing his own charity golf tournament," said Violet.

"Is he in the cabin?" asked Benny.

"I think so," said Henry. "Let's go tell Madison."

The Aldens walked down the trail to where Madison was taking pictures. They told her what they had seen.

"You found Matthew Donovan!" said Madison.

"Well, we didn't see him," said Henry.

"We saw golf clubs," said Jessie.

"It must be him," said Madison. "That man is always playing golf. He even plays in his office."

"In his office?" repeated Benny.

"Crazy, isn't it?" replied Madison. "Where did you see him? I mean, where did you see the golf clubs?"

"At the old fishing lodge," said Henry.

"Let's go," said Madison. She took her cell phone out of her pocket. "There's one way to find out if Matthew Donovan is inside."

"What is that?" asked Violet.

"We can call him!" said Madison.

Madison and the children walked down the trail to the clearing by the old fishing lodge. Then Madison called the number she had for Matthew Donovan.

Inside the cabin, they could hear a phone ringing.

Madison hung up. "I have to call Sheriff Briggs," said Madison. She quickly called the sheriff's department.

"Sheriff Briggs," said Madison. "I have some good news."

The Aldens waited with Madison until the sheriff and his three deputies arrived. They walked into the woods, and a few minutes later, Sheriff Briggs was with Matthew Donovan, who wore handcuffs.

Madison took her notebook and her pen out of her pocket. She went up to the millionaire and started asking questions.

"Did you spend all of the investors' money, Donovan? Is that why you were hiding in the woods dressed in a zombie costume, so no one could find you? And why did you tear up the grass here?" She pointed at the clumps of grass next to the trail. "Did you think we wouldn't notice?"

"Madison said he was making her crazy," said Jessie.

"Now he's making news," said Henry.

"I'll record it for her," said Violet. She walked over and filmed Madison talking to Matthew Donovan.

"Now wait a minute!" said Donovan. "Everyone makes divots when they play golf. The club pulls up a bit of dirt and grass when it swings. I was just playing a little night golf."

"Dressed as a zombie?" said Madison.

"Everyone knows about the zombie legend at this lodge," said Donovan. "I heard it when I was only a child, like them." He looked over at the Aldens. "I was just having a little fun."

Donovan leaned forward and stared at

Madison. "Why are you bothering me? I came here to get away from nosy reporters like you."

"So you *were* hiding from your investors," said Madison.

"I'm not hiding," said Donovan. "I didn't steal the investors' money. It's all just a misunderstanding."

"I don't think your investors would agree," replied Madison.

"No, they don't," said Sheriff Briggs. "That's why we're here." Then Sheriff Briggs and his deputies took Matthew Donovan away.

Madison took out her cell phone and called her editor. "I have your front page story for tomorrow," said Madison. Then she turned and looked at Violet. "And some news footage, too."

That night, Violet's film was on the news, and the next morning, Madison's story was on the front page of the *Greenfield Gazette* with one of Violet's photos. Even the teens woke up early that morning. They were huddled over a copy of the newspaper at the end of the table.

"So there isn't really a zombie," said Benny.

"No," said Jake. "It's just an old story."

Ring! Ring!

"There it goes again," said Maude. She stood up and walked into the lobby to answer the phone.

"The phone has been ringing all morning," said Jessie.

"Everyone wants to come and see where the missing millionaire was hiding out," said Jake. "Thanks to you, it looks like business is picking up."

"Glad we could help," said Henry.

"Can we see your zombie movie?" asked Jessie.

"Sure," said Jake. "We call it *The Zombie Project.* I posted it online last night."

"You put it online?" said Violet.

"Then everyone can see it," said Jake. "We made the movie to help Grandma. We wanted more people to know about the lodge."

"That's right," said Abby. She put her arm

around Jake.

Jake gave Abby a kiss. "Let me go get my laptop," said Jake. "It's in my room." He walked out of the dining room.

"I'll make the popcorn," said Abby, and she went into the kitchen.

"Popcorn!" said Benny. "Yum!"

"For breakfast?" said Jessie.

"It's a special occasion," said Violet.

"It's not every day that you catch a zombie," said Henry.

Caleb stood up and put his hands out in front of him. Then he grimaced and began walking slowly across the dining room floor. "Uh-uh-uh!" he said.

Benny ran over and grabbed Caleb by the waist.

"You got me!" said Caleb.

The Aldens laughed.